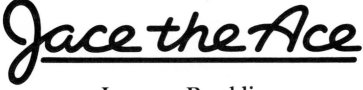

Jace the Ace

Joanne Rocklin

Illustrated by
Diane deGroat

Macmillan Publishing Company
New York

Collier Macmillan Canada
Toronto

Maxwell Macmillan International Publishing Group
New York   Oxford   Singapore   Sydney

Macmillan Publishing Company
866 Third Avenue, New York, NY 10022
Collier Macmillan Canada, Inc.
1200 Eglinton Avenue East
Suite 200
Don Mills, Ontario M3C 3N1
First Edition
Printed in the United States of America

10 9 8 7 6 5 4 3 2 1

The text of this book is set in 13 point Baskerville.
The illustrations are rendered in pencil.

Library of Congress Cataloging-in-Publication Data
Rocklin, Joanne.
Jace the Ace / Joanne Rocklin ; illustrated by Diane deGroat.   p.   cm.
Summary: When ten-year-old Jason moves from New York to Los Angeles,
he finds himself telling wildly exaggerated stories about being a
junior photojournalist and investigative reporter.
ISBN 0-02-777445-7
[1. Los Angeles (Calif.)—Fiction. 2. Honesty—Fiction.
3. Photojournalism—Fiction. 4. Moving, Household—Fiction.]
I. De Groat, Diane, ill. II. Title.
PZ7.R59Jac 1990   [Fic]—dc20   90-34095 CIP AC

For Gerry

1

Jason Caputo was on assignment in the Los Angeles Public Library. He smiled secretly to himself. To most observers, he was just an ordinary ten-year-old boy. Brown hair. Brown eyes. A boy falling below the midpoint of the boys' physical growth chart at the pediatrician's, to Jason's great disappointment.

But to those in the know, he was Jace the Ace, junior photojournalist. Unfortunately, hardly anybody knew, because Jason, his five-year-old brother, Earl, and their mother had moved to Los Angeles only that summer.

Jason trained his camera on an elderly lady reading a magazine at a nearby table. His keen eye for detail noted her gold bracelets and big diamond ring. Ah-ha, he said to himself, imagining the newspaper headline: Rich Heiress with Amnesia Discovered in Library! Jace the Ace snapped the picture.

A stern man in a business suit was using the copy machine to duplicate pages from a heavy, important-looking book. Counterintelligence Spy

Stealing Secrets from Local Library! Jace the Ace snapped the picture.

Across the table from him, a tall young man sat reading. He needed a shave, and he wore a ponytail tied with a shoelace. An arrow-shaped scar on his sunburned forehead wriggled when he scowled at his book. Jace the Ace scrutinized him carefully. What a mean-looking varmint, he thought. As mean as they come. Escaped Convict Holed Up in Library! This would be a big, big story.

The man turned a page of his book and frowned in concentration. He was reading a Puffy Bear book, Jason realized with great surprise.

Very, very suspicious. Jason sat up straighter in his chair, pretending to read his own book but watching the man's every move. He noticed that the man stared at the page for a long time, mouthing words. His finger moved along the lines, and he occasionally rubbed his grizzled beard.

Ah-ha, thought Jason. Of course. He was receiving a coded message from an accomplice.

The Puffy Bear book was the one called *Puffy Bear Rides the Big Wave*. Jason knew it well. It was one of his little brother Earl's favorite books. Jason had to admit that he himself had enjoyed it once and still had a certain fondness for it.

The Escaped Convict began to read page one. Jason mouthed the words with him. "Puffy Bear went to the seashore. He saw the waves. He wished and wished he could swim."

There was a message in there somewhere, Jason just knew it.

Then the Escaped Convict looked up as Miss Whitestreet, the librarian, stopped by their table. "How're you doing, Sky?" she asked.

"Hey, I'm trying, Miss," he said.

"Good," said Miss Whitestreet. "Let me know if you need help."

Miss Whitestreet smiled at Jason and went back to her desk. The man named Sky went back to his story, soon to discover that Puffy Bear jumps on the magic wave, which carries him far and wide on wondrous and spine-tingling adventures.

Jason sighed. Wondrous and spine-tingling adventures didn't come easily in real life. He should know, because he looked for them all the time. How did a boy get to be a star reporter, anyway? Jason looked at his camera, lying on the table in front of him. It was an old one that used to belong to his dad, who had died when Jason was six years old. Jason longed to put it to good use, but he couldn't even afford to put film in it most of the time. And anyway, only kids in books and on TV got to be detectives and ace reporters and have exciting things happen to them.

Except for that one time at the beginning of the summer. Jason remembered how wonderful it had been. He had helped Sonia Begley with her business, S.S.S.S. (Sonia's Safety Sentinel Service, a house-watching service for vacationers). Then a reporter named Al "Deadline" Hernandez had interviewed them and taken their picture for the newspaper. Boy, had that felt good!

"I'm in training to be a photojournalist, too," he had said to Al.

"Zat so?" Al had held his camera sideways to get a better shot of Jason standing proud and feeling tall.

"Yes," Jason had said. "Any tips?"

Al had thought for a moment and said, "Sure, son. Jot these down."

Jason had whipped his little notebook and pencil from his back pocket.

"Number one," Al had said. "There are stories all around you. Big ones. Wallapalloozas. Keep the old eye, ear, and nose ever on the alert."

"Big stories. Got it."

"Number two. The old camera never lies."

"Old camera never lies. *My* camera's very old."

Al had chuckled. "Just a figure of speech, son.

Old cameras, new cameras, they never lie."

"Got it."

"Number three. Very important. The pen is powerful." Al had gestured at Jason's pencil stub. "Also pencils, crayons, typewriters, and burned matchsticks. Anything that writes."

"Got it." Jason had scribbled furiously. Then Al had given him his card. Jason felt honored to be given tips by an expert and he knew he would never forget them.

Jason had bought twenty copies of the *West L.A. Public Weekly* with his picture in it and the story by Al "Deadline" Hernandez. He had mailed a big pile of the newspapers to his relatives and his best buddy, Mikey, in New York City. He'd kept Al's card in his wallet and carried it everywhere he went.

So big deal. Jason sighed again. That was old, old news already. Sonia Begley had disbanded her business because the summer vacation was just about over. Now she spent all her time with her best friend, Mary Anne, who had returned from visiting her grandmother in Idaho.

And Mikey. Jason sighed, thinking about his old friend from his old neighborhood.

"Dear Jace," Mikey had written. "Thanks for the newspapers. Sounds like you are having a fun time. Nothing new or special is happening around here since you left. I'm okay, I guess. They make a lot of movies and TV shows out there, don't they? Seen anyone famous yet?"

"Dear Mikey," Jason had responded. "Good to hear from you! You should see this place. The sun shines practically all the time in Los Angeles, which everybody calls L.A. for short. Funny-looking palm trees stand around almost everywhere you look. Birds are so colorful they look like flowers in the trees, and some flowers, called bird-of-paradise, look like birds. Nothing exciting has happened lately. I have seen nobody famous yet."

Jason had written over and over again to Mikey. He told him everything. He told him that he lived on Lemon Grove Avenue but that there were no lemon groves anywhere. He told him that the star constellations couldn't be seen very well from his bedroom window and that a huge, flashing neon sign lit up the sky at night. *Orange Fizz, The Drink that Kids Love!* it said, which wasn't true, because he didn't. He told Mikey about his trip to the zoo, swimming in the ocean, and roller-skating on the beach walks. And when he ran out of things to say he made up a funny story about a big black dog, just the kind of dog he and his brother wanted.

And today he had finally received Mikey's reply.

Jason pulled it out of his pocket and read it again.

"Dear Jace," Mikey had written. "Nothing new or special is happening around here since you left. I'm okay, I guess. Hope you are, too. Seen anybody famous yet?"

Jason sighed again. He didn't really care if nothing was new. He would have been glad to hear about old things.

He picked up his camera and stared through it, framing with the camera eye the man named Sky. Escaped Convict Holed Up in Library!

How he wished it were true. After alerting the proper authorities, he would write the story, be interviewed himself and probably photographed. Everybody would speak of Jace the Ace in hushed, respectful voices. New kids would want to know him, old friends would never forget him.

Sky looked up from his book. "Hey, kid, make sure I get a copy of that picture."

Jason reddened. "I didn't really take it," he said. "No film."

"Well, if you ever do, I want a copy. To send home to Mom."

Jason tried to imagine this mean-looking varmint with a mom, the kind who worried about him if he didn't wear a jacket or who sang lullabies to him at night. It wasn't easy. Would she put her

scowling son's picture on the nightstand as his own mom did the photographs of Jason and Earl?

Sky went back to his book. He frowned, making his scar-arrow dance.

Jason remembered his own worries about Puffy Bear, and how relieved he had been when Puffy Bear finally had learned to swim. But he had been five years old, for goodness' sake!

Jason glanced at his watch. His mother would be just about getting off work by now. "Let's go home, Earl," he said to his brother, who was looking at a picture book and pretending to read it. "It's almost time for Captain Lightning."

"Captain Lightning's Interplanetary Adventures" was their favorite TV show. It was Mikey's favorite show, too, but Mikey had already seen his episode for the day because they were three hours ahead in New York. Jason felt as if he himself were on a different planet.

The rich heiress was making a phone call, her memory returned. The counterintelligence spy was reading to a little boy on his lap. The escaped convict was a man named Sky who liked to read Puffy Bear books. And *he,* Jason thought mournfully, slipping his camera strap over his head, was just a short, ordinary kid without a good buddy. He gathered together his library books to check out, books he had already read but wanted to read again. At least the books were old friends.

"Come back soon, Jason," said Miss White-street, stamping his books. She always remembered his name.

A teenage boy was entering the library as Jason and Earl were walking out. His hair was shaved off on one side of his head, and dyed purple and green on the other.

Extraterrestrials Invade Local Library!

Jace the Ace snapped the picture.

2

A black dog was lying on the library steps. The dog had been there when the boys had entered the building. He sniffed Jason's outstretched hand cheerfully. He was just the kind of dog Jason wished they had. Large and friendly and kind of messy looking, a dog who would romp along a wet beach or lead the way up a steep, dusty trail toward adventure.

"I'll bet his name is King or Sampson or Lightning," said Jason, patting his head.

"Or Superdog!" exclaimed Earl.

"It sure would be nice to come home to a dog like that," said Jason. He slowed his steps, remembering who was really waiting in their backyard.

Poopsie. Poopsie, with his little bow perched on top of his head and his little clickety-clackety toenails and round tail, so unlike the library dog. Poopsie, the French poodle who belonged to Mrs. Raski, their grouchy downstairs landlady. The very first words Mrs. Raski had said to Jason and Earl when she met them, Jason remembered, were not hello, nice to meet you. As soon as she saw two brothers jumping out of the big U-Haul driven by their mother all the way from New York, two boys who must have looked like they might possibly want a dog, she said, "The backyard has always belonged to Poopsie. No other pets allowed!"

Jason had wanted to move somewhere else even before they'd unpacked their U-Haul. But his mother had said that the rent was right, at least until their ship came in. She had said that because of her new job with a higher salary there was a better chance that their ship would come in on the Pacific Ocean than the Atlantic, but they still had to count every penny. And having an adult on the premises when Jason and Earl came home alone on school days would give her some peace of mind.

"A witch on the premises," Jason had said. A witch who watched their every move from her window or her squeaky front-porch rocker, and banged on the ceiling with her witch's broom if they played the TV too loudly.

Thinking these sorry thoughts, Jason hurried home to watch his favorite TV program. Earl scurried beside him, trying to keep up.

Suddenly a tall, lone figure ahead caught Jason's eye. A man with long legs, swinging his arms purposefully as if off on a great adventure, was striding down the street.

Jason could hardly believe it! It was the star of the very show they were hurrying home to watch! He was sure of it. Those legs, that long, sure stride, that brave head held aloft by thoughts of adventure!

"Earl, look!" he said excitedly. "Isn't that Captain Lightning?"

"Where?" asked Earl, looking around with interest. "Where?"

"Up ahead! You can't see him very well now, but it's him, it really is!"

"Hey, Captain!" shouted Earl.

"Fearless and dauntless, exploring new vistas and the mysteries of the planets and galaxies, I will prevail!" Jason shouted the familiar opening refrain of the show, hoping the Captain would recognize it and turn around.

But the Captain didn't hear them. "Hurry up, Earl," said Jason. "Let's try to catch up to him!"

Oh, how he wanted to talk to the Captain! "Dear Mikey," he would write. "I met somebody famous today." And he would get Captain Lightning's autograph and make a copy of it to mail to Mikey. Maybe he would even send him the *original*, for Mikey would appreciate and cherish it as much as Jason would.

Jason and Earl quickened their pace as the man began to walk even faster. Captain Lightning turned left and headed toward the park. Jason and Earl followed close behind, around a picnic area, across a baseball field, up and down a winding jogging path.

"I'm tired," said Earl, panting.

Phooey! thought Jason. Here he was, about to meet somebody famous, and Earl was spoiling everything.

"Go sit on that park bench," he ordered. "And don't move until I get back."

Jason raced ahead. There, in front of him, the Captain had begun to do leg stretches. From behind a tree, Jason watched. Then the man began to do jumping jacks. One-two, one-two.

Jason planned to speak to him right after the scissor jumps. Hi, I'm known as Jace the Ace, he would say. May I please ask you a few questions?

"Excuse me, Captain!" Jason called, running determinedly with his head down.

The man stopped jumping and turned around.

Jason tripped on his shoelace and fell, sprawled at the man's feet.

"Hey, what do you think you're doing, kid?" an angry voice asked.

Jason looked up. Staring down at him was an unfamiliar face with a long nose and a bristling mustache.

"I'm really sorry, mister," he said sheepishly. "I thought you were someone else." He picked himself up off the ground. Then a thought occurred to him. "You wouldn't happen to be famous, would you?"

The man smiled, his mustache twitching. He glanced at Jason's camera strung around his neck. "Sorry, no," he said. Then he turned and continued jogging down the path.

Jason picked up his library books from the ground. His skinned knee poked through a tear in his jeans, jeans that he knew his mother hoped Earl would inherit in one piece. Oh, Jace, his mom was going to say, why are you always getting carried away by your imagination?

Earl was still sitting on the park bench. "Did you get his autograph?" he asked tearfully.

"No. He said he was in a hurry," said Jason, ashamed to admit the truth of his silly mistake, even to Earl. "Oh, stop bawling. I wasn't gone that long."

They had entered an unfamiliar section of the park. Jason chose a jogging path and trudged down it with Earl sniffling quietly beside him. They followed the path until it emerged onto a sidewalk bordering a big, busy street. Jason didn't know whether to turn left or right. He waved at a passing police car, which pulled over to the curb.

"You guys tourists?" asked the officer in the driver's seat, leaning out the window and gesturing toward Jason's camera.

"No," said Jason. "But we're kind of new in town. We came out of the park at the wrong end."

"Hop in," said the officer. "I'm Officer Jordan, and this is my partner, Officer Brown. We'll drive you home."

"Are we being arrested?" asked Earl worriedly as they got into the backseat.

"No, silly," said Jason. He gave their address on Lemon Grove Avenue, and the police car drove off. Soon they passed the minimall in their neighborhood and the *Drink that Kids Love!* sign that Jason could see from his bedroom window.

"Turn left at the next block," he told the officers.

The police radio crackled mysterious messages, and the officers' badges glinted importantly. Jason leaned against the backseat, enjoying the ride.

His mother, Mrs. Raski, and Poopsie were standing on the street in front of his house as the police car drove up.

"Hi, everybody!" Jason shouted. He and Earl hopped out of the car with the officers.

"We were worried about you!" cried his mother.

Earl hugged her. "Mama, we were chasing after Captain Lightning, but he was in a hurry and we came out on the wrong end of the park," he said.

"Oh, Jace," said his mother. "Why are you always getting carried away by your imagination?"

"I might have known," said Mrs. Raski, and Poopsie barked his own disapproval.

"I wanted to interview him and get his autograph," explained Jason.

"Your son did have enough sense to flag us down and ask us for help," said Officer Brown.

Suddenly Jason had an idea. "Can you wait just a minute?" he asked the officers.

Jason raced upstairs. Quickly, he loaded his camera with film he'd been saving for something important or exciting, like a news assignment or a trip to Disneyland, whichever came first. He raced downstairs again.

"Please take our picture. For a souvenir," he said to his mother, handing her the camera.

Dear Mikey,
CONFIDENTIAL:

I have just spent some time with a couple of my new buddies, Officer Jordan and Officer

Brown. I gave them some information and some direction on an important case. Photos to follow.

> I remain,
> Your old buddy,
> Jace the Ace
> Junior Photojournalist

3

The letter wasn't *really* lying, Jason reasoned. That's what he had said to himself as he wrote it one lonely Saturday. That's what he had said to himself when he put a stamp on the envelope and mailed it. But when he heard the soft *whoosh* of the letter sliding down the dark hole of the mailbox, he knew that he was telling himself a lie, too.

Several times Jason tried to telephone Al "Deadline" Hernandez at the *West L.A. Public Weekly.* Maybe he could be signed up as a junior photojournalist right away, to make the letter less of a lie.

"Mr. Hernandez is on another line, Mr. Caputo," his secretary, Judy, always said.

"May I hold?" Jason asked.

"It will probably be a while, sir. I'd be glad to take a message."

"Tell him it's Jason Caputo. Jace the Ace. I worked with him on a case this summer. You have my number."

"Will do, Jace," said Judy.

So far, Mr. Hernandez had not returned his

calls. Jason was disappointed, but he understood. Mr. Hernandez probably had a zillion phone calls to return, every single day, what with all the important information he was gathering.

Meanwhile, Jason continued to look for stories to report and mysteries to solve. Nothing much was happening on Lemon Grove Avenue, except that Mrs. Caputo's morning newspaper was occasionally missing from the front porch.

"Drat! Missing again!" she exclaimed one morning just before school began. "I'll have to report this to the newspaper office."

Jason snapped pictures of the scene of the crime. He looked for fingerprints and telltale clues, but there were none. Mr. Hernandez would be interested in this, if only Jason could get through to him.

His mother watched him, smiling. "It's probably just an administrative mix-up, honey. Save your film for Disneyland." Then she kissed her sons good-bye for the day. "Mrs. Raski will give you lunch."

Jason and Earl wrinkled up their noses at each other. The smell of stew was coming from Mrs. Raski's kitchen.

"Dog stew," Jason said. "She's making us the same stuff she gives to Poopsie!"

"Ugh!" agreed Earl.

"Don't be silly," said Mrs. Caputo. "It's perfectly good stew. Giving some of it to Poopsie doesn't make it dog stew." Then she hopped into her car to brave the crowded freeways, which made her come home later than she used to.

The boys watched some TV and then got dressed and went outside. At the end of Lemon Grove Avenue, Sonia and Mary Anne were standing on the corner. Sonia played her guitar and Mary Anne shook a tambourine while they crooned a duet. They had recently begun a new business, S.S.S., or Serenading Sitter Sisters. S.S.S. hoped to become famous one day, perhaps after being discovered by a director or a producer while Sonia and Mary Anne were singing lullabies to the director's or producer's children, or just singing on the corner.

Jason had wanted to join S.S.S. But Mary Anne had pointed out that he didn't know how to play an instrument and, being a boy, couldn't possibly be a Sister.

"Doo-dah, doo-dah," S.S.S. sang. "Since I fell for you-oo, you broke my heart in two-oo. . . ."

Jason and Earl stopped to listen. Sonia had her eyes closed. Mary Anne shook her head back and forth as hard as she shook the tambourine.

"Hi, guys!" said Sonia, opening her eyes when their song was done.

"Are you going to take our picture?" asked Mary Anne, patting her hair. Her hair was tied in a ponytail on the left side of her head. Sonia's hair was tied in a ponytail on the right side.

"I'm saving my camera for news," he said.

"*We're* news!" said Mary Anne. "We're going to be rich and famous one day."

"Jason doesn't even have film in his camera," said Sonia, giggling.

"I do so!" said Jason hotly.

"Hey, you don't have to get mad," said Sonia. But she and Mary Anne began giggling again.

"Stop laughing!" cried Earl. "My brother has lots and lots of film in his camera!"

"Prove it!" said Mary Anne.

Jason couldn't resist a bet when he knew he would win. He snapped a picture of the two girls laughing into the camera.

"Let's go, Earl," he said haughtily. Everybody thought he was so darn funny.

It was going to be a long day. The mailman had already come and gone, dashing Jason's hopes of receiving a letter from Mikey. Jason followed Earl into the backyard. Earl wanted to check up on a plump snail that lived behind a juniper bush.

At the far end of the yard, in front of his dog-house, Poopsie observed both boys with obvious distaste. Jason sat down on the grass and glared back at Poopsie.

"How're you doing, Mr. Snail?" Earl asked, kneeling beside the juniper bush. "Hey, Jace, what are those two squiggly things sticking up on its head?"

"Antennae, I think."

"Like TV antennas?"

"Sort of. They help the snail feel around and see better."

Earl poked his face closer to his pet. "Hi, Uncle Seymour," he said.

"That's his name?"

Earl nodded solemnly. "He can see more than you think, so he's Uncle Seymour."

"You're a weirdo, Earl," said Jason.

Still, he had to give Earl credit. Even though Mrs. Raski had said no more pets allowed, Earl didn't listen, no sirree. By last count there was Bernie Beetle, Caw-Caw the Crow, and Wendy Worm. And now there was Uncle Seymour. Poopsie was outnumbered.

Poopsie, who had shown an interest in the snail since Earl had befriended it, was growling and stealthily creeping across the lawn.

Earl looked up. "Go away, you!" he shouted.

A window was opened, and Mrs. Raski leaned her head out. "Boys, I've told you before, *please* don't tease Poopsie. He's got a weak heart and hasn't been feeling very well lately!"

"We're not teasing him!" cried Earl.

"Well, be gentle, please. He's very sensitive!"

She banged the window shut. Earl stuck out his tongue at Poopsie.

"Please don't tease Poopsie!" said Jason in a squeaky voice, imitating Mrs. Raski.

"I don't care!" said Earl defiantly. He turned back to his snail. "Jace, isn't Uncle Seymour smart to carry his house around on his back so he never ever has to move?"

"Seems like a good idea to me," said Jason.

"Do snails sleep?" asked Earl. "How can they recognize their own mother or brother? Do snails know when they're going in the wrong direction, or do they just keep going?"

Jason knew what Earl's next question would be. "Can we go to the library, Jace?"

At the library Earl chose a book called *All About Snails.* Jason decided on a mystery, always good for a thrill when things were slow and dreary.

At the far end of the reading table, the mysterious Sky was sitting beside another man. Jason noticed that they were reading the same book together.

"That's enough for today," said the man to Sky, patting him on the back. "I think we're starting to crack the code, don't you?"

Jason began to listen attentively.

"The Big Twenty-six is a tough code to crack," said Sky.

What a strange conversation, thought Jason. Could it be that these men were undercover agents, undercover cops, undercover anythings, sitting right in his very own neighborhood library?

"We'll meet again, same time and place," the other man said. He picked up a big briefcase and left.

Code Big Twenty-six, Jason wrote in his little notebook. He would need some more information.

"Your kids are really going to like that book," Jason commented, noticing that Sky was reading the Puffy Bear book again.

Sky looked up. "What?" he asked in a gruff voice.

"I said your kids are going to like that book. My brother and I do."

Sky smiled. "Don't have any kids," he said.

"Oh. Well, do *you* like it?"

Sky flipped through the pages of the little book. "Yes, I do," he said. "Still like to ride the waves myself, every now and then." He pointed to a picture of Puffy Bear with hat and spectacles askew, only his umbrella keeping him afloat. "But I'll tell you one thing: This dude better learn to swim if he doesn't want to drown."

"I notice that you come here a lot," said Jason. "Do you work in the neighborhood?"

"I work nights in a restaurant nearby. Helps pay my library fines," said Sky, winking.

Jason decided to get right to the point. "That code you were talking about with your friend. Are you free to discuss it?"

"What code?"

"You know. The Big Twenty-six."

Sky's face got very red. "Figure it out for yourself, kid," he said. Then he pulled a newspaper from an old orange sack and began to read, ignoring Jason.

Definitely hiding something, Jason decided. The world was full of stories, just like Al "Deadline" Hernandez said. Also grouches.

When Jason and Earl left the library, the same dog was sitting on the library stairs, as he had been when the boys went in. Jason patted his head, and he licked Jason's hand.

At the thought of dogs and dog stew for lunch, Jason bought two doughnuts for himself and Earl at the Donut Dunk in the minimall. He could hear Poopsie barking excitedly as he always did when the boys passed the *Drink that Kids Love!* sign at the corner of Lemon Grove Avenue. When Jason unlocked the backyard gate, the dog was hovering near the juniper bush, shivering with intensity.

Too late, Jason realized what was about to happen. "No!" he yelled.

"Uncle Seymour!" shouted Earl at the same time.

But with a yelp and a growl, Poopsie pounced upon the unlucky snail.

"Poopsie!" cried Mrs. Raski, rushing out of her house. Poopsie whimpered piteously when he saw his owner. Mrs. Raski ran to her dog and picked him up.

"Oh, my poor, poor baby!" she cried. "You'll be sick now and vomit all through the night!" She carried the poodle into her house, murmuring into the dog's gray ear solicitously, as if Poopsie himself had been the victim of the attack.

The boys ran to the snail. Its handsome shell was crushed, and Uncle Seymour was quite dead.

Jason was surprised, for it had never occurred to him that his brother's snail was in danger. He knew that snails were eaten in French restaurants by people, but not that they were eaten by French poodles.

"Uncle Seymour's not moving," said Earl tearfully.

"Poopsie killed him, Earl," said Jason.

Earl cradled his pet in his two palms. "Are you sure?"

"I'm sure," said Jason. "We have to bury him." He pulled a crumpled tissue from the pocket of his jeans and wrapped up the dead snail.

"Good-bye, Uncle Seymour. You were a good friend," said Earl over the snail's little grave when they were done. "I hate Poopsie a lot, Jace."

"So do I," said Jason, who never thought he'd meet a dog he didn't like.

Jason and Earl sat down beside the grave. Jason read stories to his brother, postponing *All About Snails* for a happier time.

Dear Mikey,
CONFIDENTIAL:

There are several mysterious characters in our neighborhood, some of whom I am questioning.

I was witness to a murder on our property recently. The victim was known as Uncle Seymour.

> I remain,
> Your old buddy,
> Jace the Ace
> Junior Photojournalist

4

Once, Jason remembered, he and Mikey had bought some bubble gum. First they'd chewed it nice and soft, swallowing all the sugar. Then they'd begun to blow big, pink, wonderful bubbles. Mikey's bubble had popped first, but Jason's had continued to grow and grow. A crowd of kids had gathered, and when the bubble finally burst all over his face and hair, the crowd had cheered. He'd had to get a haircut, but it had been worth it.

His lie was like that bubble-gum bubble, growing and growing. But it sure wasn't as much fun.

The day before school began, Jason received a letter from Mikey. It was the longest letter Mikey had ever written him, and probably anyone else.

"Wow! A murder!" Mikey wrote. "Was there much blood? Who was the person who got killed? I hope you are okay. You must live in a very dangerous part of town. Nothing special happening around here. Write back ASAP. (Don't worry. I'll keep it confidential)."

Jason read the letter over and over again. He wanted to respond as soon as possible, but he didn't know what to write.

"I see you got a letter from Mikey," his mother commented the next day at breakfast. "What does he have to say?"

"Not much," said Jason, guiltily folding up the letter and putting it in his pocket.

"Give my best regards to Mikey's parents," said Mrs. Caputo, looking at her watch and getting up from the table. "Hurry up, kids. I have to get you to school a bit earlier on the first day. Gather your things together." She glanced at Jason's camera, which was sitting on top of his knapsack by his chair. "Why are you taking your camera?"

"I'm training to be a photojournalist, Mom," said Jason. "You know that." It seemed that he had to remind his mother daily.

"Plenty of time to train after school," said Mrs. Caputo, frowning. "Remember those new leaves we talked about turning over?"

Jason sighed. Comments from old report cards swirled in his memory: Daydreams too much. Needs to improve concentration. Bright boy with imagination not working to potential.

Across from Jason, Earl was sniffling. Tears dropped into his bowl of cereal. "I don't want to go to kinnergarden! I want to stay with Jason!"

"Oh, honey," said Mrs. Caputo. "Jason will pick you up at your door the very minute your after-school day care is over. Maybe he'll even take you to the library."

Jason suddenly grabbed Earl's new yellow lunch box with its picture of Monster Man on the front. "Aargh!" he shouted. "I want to go to kindergarten! Earl must take me to kindergarten, or else!"

Earl began to giggle through his tears. "Oh, yeah, I forgot. Monster Man wants to learn how to read. Okay, I'll try it out."

Mrs. Caputo leaned over to wipe Earl's teary face with a napkin. "Thanks, Jace," she said.

Jason understood how Earl felt about his new lunch box. Earl liked it so much that he slept with it. Sometimes Jason felt the same way about his camera, although he wouldn't go so far as to sleep with it.

"My camera will start lots of conversations with the other kids, Mom," said Jason, slowly beginning to put the camera into its case.

Mrs. Caputo looked at him for a few seconds. "Oh, all right, take it," she said. "But no major flights of fancy when you look through its lens, okay?"

"Okay," promised Jason.

When they arrived at Palm Street Elementary School, Mrs. Caputo registered her sons at the office and then took Earl to the kindergarten room. Jason found Miss McFeen's room, the fifth-grade class to which he had been assigned. All the other fifth graders were exchanging hearty greetings, as if they had known one another for years and years.

Jason chose a seat by the window, placing his camera in front of him on his desk. Then he took out his new loose-leaf notebook and freshly sharpened pencils from his knapsack.

A boy sitting beside him leaned toward Jason's desk. "I'm Paul. Great camera," he said.

Jason thanked Paul and introduced himself. Conversation number one.

A boy sitting in front of Jason turned around, scrutinized the camera, and remarked, "It's not so great. My father has a much newer model. He lets me use it all the time!"

Conversation number two, thought Jason. Sort of.

After marking attendance and collecting the lunch money, Miss McFeen got right down to business.

"Today we will review the reduction of fractions," she said.

Jason chose one of his pencils and opened his loose-leaf notebook.

"First, as you may remember, you must find the common denominator," said Miss McFeen, writing on the chalkboard.

Jason tried to listen attentively and concentrate. He was determined to turn over his new leaf. A new leaf just like the big, fat palm frond, crisp and green, on the palm tree right outside the window.

"Divide the common denominator into the numerator," Miss McFeen continued, her chalk squeaking.

Such a funny tree, thought Jason. So different from the trees he was used to. And its leaves never fell off, unlike the leaves that soon would be changing color in his old neighborhood.

Jason continued to stare out the window. He had begun to think about snow and had gone on to remember snowball fights with a good buddy and Christmas, when he was suddenly startled out of his reverie.

A shadowy figure was scurrying across the schoolyard! It quickly darted behind the palm tree.

Jason craned his neck to get a closer look. He saw a bright flash of something yellow. To the untrained eye, he thought, the scene was innocent. A palm tree. A schoolyard. An open window. But to those in the know, to those ever alert to big stories, this could mean only one thing!

Spy Stalks School, Seeks Math Secrets.

Miss McFeen's back was turned. Slowly, ever so slowly, Jason picked up his camera. Peering through the lens he saw another flash of yellow.

Jace the Ace snapped the picture.

"Hey, Josh!"

The whispered warning from Paul had come too late. Miss McFeen's chalk was no longer squeaking, for she had stopped reducing her fractions. All eyes were on Jason.

"Please bring that camera to me," said Miss McFeen sternly. Jason, red-faced, shuffled to the front of the room and handed it to her.

When he went back to his seat, the "spy" was waiting. It was Earl, poking his head through the window. "Monster Man wants to go home now," he said.

"Go back!" whispered Jason through clenched teeth.

"You come to kinnergarden with me, then!" shouted Earl.

"Go with him, Jason," said Miss McFeen with a sigh.

Jason sat on a little chair beside Earl in the

kindergarten room. They sang songs about spiders and parts of the body. They played with blocks and fed the guinea pigs and finger painted. At lunch, a happier Earl and a girl named Jennifer traded sandwiches from their Monster Man lunch boxes. Jason was told he could return to his own room.

"The Kindergarten Kid is back!" shouted the boy whose father had the better camera.

"That's enough, Andrew," said Miss McFeen.

In the schoolyard, Jason stood alone as children cheerfully swirled about him. Andrew and Paul came over to him, dribbling a basketball between them.

"Too bad about your camera, Josh," said Paul. "Miss McFeen is very strict. Last year's fifth graders called her Mean Lean McFeen. They say she's a very hard grader."

"My name's Jason. Or Jace," corrected Jason.

"Or Kindergarten Kid!" said Andrew.

Jason flushed. It had not been an entirely unpleasant morning in the kindergarten, but that didn't mean he belonged there!

"Oh, cut it out, Andy," said Paul. "Hey, why'd you bring your camera to school, anyway?"

"I'm training," said Jason. And then Jason pulled Mr. Hernandez's card from his pocket and said out loud something he had said only to himself. Because of course it really wasn't true.

"I work with this guy," Jason said.

"Wow!" said Paul. "At the *West L.A. Public Weekly*? What do you do?"

"Official junior photojournalist," said Jason.

After lunch Miss McFeen pulled down a map of the United States in front of the chalkboard and began to review the states and their capitals. Sacramento, California. Lincoln, Nebraska. Albany, New York. Jason stared at the Pacific Ocean and the Atlantic Ocean and the thousands and thousands of miles in between. How he missed having a buddy!

Then Jason opened his notebook to a fresh page and began to write. He wrote and wrote, the sentences tumbling out of him and seeming to bump into each other on the page. When he had finished, he felt satisfied. It was a wonderful letter. A wallapallooza.

Miss McFeen rolled up the map. "Now we will have a quiz," she announced.

Gasps filled the room. "Oh, come on now," she said. "It will be a short fill-in-the-blanks. If you were paying attention, you should do fine."

Miss McFeen passed out the tests. Jason did the

best he could, considering that he hadn't really paid much attention. Miss McFeen began to patrol the rows of students. As she paused at his desk, Jason covered his letter with his hand. Could she have seen any of it? he wondered.

At the end of the day, Miss McFeen unlocked her drawer and returned Jason's camera to him. "There's no need to bring this to class," she said. "I'll tell you when you can use it again. And in case you missed anything in the fraction review, you may do extra practice, page fourteen, for tomorrow."

Jason wrote down the extra homework in his little notebook, under his notes about the mysterious Sky and the missing newspapers.

"And here is today's quiz, already graded," continued Miss McFeen. Her long red fingernail pointed to the big red D minus at the top of the page. "Have it signed by your mother, please, and return it as soon as possible."

A D minus! "That's the lowest grade I ever got," mumbled Jason.

"You could have done better if you had been concentrating on the right things at the right time," said Miss McFeen. "Your records show that you're a bright boy with imagination who doesn't work to potential."

Then she looked at Jason with concern in her eyes. "Is everything okay at home, Jason? Are all your family members in good health?"

"They're fine," said Jason.

"I'm very relieved to hear that," said Miss McFeen with a smile.

Dear Mikey,
CONFIDENTIAL:

Uncle Seymour, the murder victim, was a nice fellow, dependable and quiet. He was killed by several sharp, pointed objects, snatched by the jaws of death before he knew what was happening. He moved too slowly—there was no time for a struggle.

The murderer was a neighbor of mine, a dog of a creature. He's not talking. I think he and Uncle Seymour were arguing over territorial rights. The murderer got locked up.

I remain,
Your old buddy,
Jace the Ace
Junior Photojournalist

5

Jason picked up Earl at his after-school day care. On the way to the library they passed Andrew and Paul.

"Hi, Josh!" said Paul.

"Hey, Kindergarten Kid!" said Andrew.

"Those are the wrong names," said Earl. "I'm Earl and he's Jason."

"Or Jace for short," said Jason, flushing.

"Sorry," said Paul. "I never remember names of new people."

"Sometimes it helps when you rhyme things," Jason offered, relieved to find out that Paul wasn't forgetting on purpose. "For instance, Jace rhymes with Ace. That's what my friend Mr. Hernandez calls me."

Paul looked impressed. "You mean that newspaperman you work for?"

"Uh, yes," said Jason.

Andrew frowned. "Let me see that guy's card again."

Jason put his hand in his pocket and pulled it out. Andrew scrutinized it carefully. "Are you really an official junior photojournalist?"

"Uh-huh," said Jason, feeling a slight twinge in his stomach.

The boys walked on together until they passed the basketball court in the park next to the library. As they ran toward the court, Paul and Andrew bounced their ball back and forth to each other.

"Hey, Jason! Catch!" called Paul. He threw the ball in a wide arc toward Jason. Jason, surprised, dropped his knapsack, reached up, and caught the ball with both hands.

"Go, go!" yelled Earl.

Jason stood still. He glanced at Paul with his arms outstretched and at Andrew, poised to run. Then he looked at the net, empty and waiting. How he wanted to plop the ball right in it! He began to run toward the net, clutching the ball to his chest.

Earl was jumping up and down. "Touchdown!" he yelled.

Jason ran as fast as he could, took aim, and shot. The ball missed the net, hitting the backboard.

"Traveling! Traveling!" shouted Paul. He ran to retrieve the ball. "You can't just run with the ball like that! Don't you even know how to dribble?"

"Not really," admitted Jason. "Basketball's not my game."

"Aw, he's too short for basketball!" said Andrew. "He's just a Kindergarten Kid!"

Earl began to defend his brother. "You keep making mistakes!" he said hotly, shaking his finger at Andrew and Paul. *"I'm* in kinnergarden. Jason's in fifth grade. And, anyway, it was a very, very good try!"

Andrew and Paul burst out laughing. Jason knew Earl was just repeating what Jason and Mrs. Caputo usually said when Earl didn't do something well, but he didn't need his little brother defending him.

"Aw, pipe down, Earl." Jason felt his face getting red again. "Anyway," he said to Andrew and Paul, "I'm too busy for basketball because of my junior photojournalist training."

"Oh, sure!" sneered Andrew. "I'll bet you're working on a case right now."

"Maybe I am," said Jason.

"Like what?" asked Andrew.

"Tracking down a ring of newspaper thieves in the neighborhood," replied Jason. At least *that* wasn't a lie.

Just then the big black dog trotted by. Beside the dog walked the man named Sky, carrying his old orange sack. The dog raced up the library steps. Jason thought he heard Sky whistle a bit of "The Star-Spangled Banner," and the dog imme-

diately lay down by the library door. Sky patted him on the head and went inside. Earl ran ahead of the boys to pat the dog, too.

"And investigating mean-looking, mysterious strangers," said Jason.

Uh-oh. He hadn't meant to say that. It had just come popping out before he could think! But then again, Sky *was* a mean-looking, mysterious stranger, wasn't he?

"Wow," said Paul.

Before they could ask any more questions, Jason pulled his camera from his knapsack. "I've got work to do in the library," he said.

Jason and Earl returned their books to Miss Whitestreet and decided on several others. Jason chose numbers ten and eleven in the series *Bobby Bipple, Boy Detective* (he had already read numbers one through nine) and a book called *Basketball: A Guidebook for Young Athletes.*

Earl chose a big pile of picture books and sat down beside Jason. "Jace, would you—" he began.

"No," said Jason, pulling out his math book. "I can't read to you. I've got a lot to do."

He was angry at Earl for embarrassing him in front of Andrew and Paul. And, besides, he must have read about a zillion books to Earl over the past four years. His mother would be cooking supper and Earl would kind of slouch in his highchair, drooling and laughing and making funny noises, hardly understanding what Jason was reading. But Jason had read and read, anyway. It had been good practice, he had to admit. "What a good reader Jason is!" his teachers had said to his mom, back in the days before teachers started complaining about him. Jason picked up his pencil. Seven books a week times fifty-two weeks in a year times the four years that he'd been reading to Earl. That equaled 1,456 books. It wasn't a zillion, but it sure was a lot. He had done his share.

Earl looked hurt. He picked up a book and began to read out loud, glancing at Jason when he came to a hard word to see if his brother noticed his struggle.

"You're doing great," Jason said.

"Puffy Bear went to kinnergarden," Earl said, pretending to read. "Mrs. Boscoe was his teacher, and Jennifer was his friend. His brother was Stinko Jason Bear."

"Very funny."

Still, Earl hadn't meant to embarrass him, thought Jason. Earl had been trying to stick up for him.

"All right," said Jason, taking Earl's book. "Just

one." It was a short bedtime alphabet story that Earl liked very much and knew by heart.

"'And the yaks yawned and the zebras z-z-z-z-d.' The end. Now you're on your own." Jason handed the book to his brother.

"'Aardvarks awaken,'" read Earl happily, turning back to the first page.

Jason did his math homework. When he had finished, he opened up the basketball book and looked at the pictures. How tall those basketball players were! He stared at the photographs for a while, sighed, and closed the book again.

Sky was sitting at the table across from them. Jason began to watch him. Sky was writing on a piece of paper. He scowled as he erased what he had written and began again, hunching his tall frame over the table.

Miss Whitestreet came over to him. "Sky," she said, "John Evans just called. He had an emergency at work and won't be able to tutor you today."

"Oh," said Sky. His shoulders sagged.

John Evans? Sky's tutor?

"'Quail are quiet, robins rest, and swordfish snooze,'" sang Earl in a loud voice so that Miss Whitestreet would hear him.

"Terrific, Earl," she said, going back to her desk.

The Big Twenty-six. All of a sudden Jason understood what the mysterious code had been. It wasn't a mysterious code at all, but just the ABC's! He had been so busy looking for exciting news, he hadn't recognized something plain and simple.

Sky put down his pencil, but he didn't seem to want to leave. He saw Jason looking at him.

"Hey, kid," he said, getting up from his seat to show his paper to Jason. "This here's a letter to my mom. I want to make sure it's okay, you know? So she understands it. Think you could look it over?"

Jason looked at the letter, a short one. "i miss you, Mom. i am O.K. Right back. Love, Sky."

"It's a good letter," said Jason. But it was true, he thought with astonishment. Sky was just learning things he himself had learned a long, long time ago.

"You have to make your *i* a big one when you talk about yourself," Jason said. "And *write* has a *W,* even though you can't hear it." Jason wrote the correct spelling on a piece of paper.

"Well, what do you know! A *W!*" exclaimed Sky, sitting down beside Jason. "Those quiet fellas keep popping up when you don't expect them, don't they? Thanks, kid."

Sky erased his mistakes and corrected them. When he was done he looked up and smiled with satisfaction, his scar-arrow dancing merrily. He glanced at Jason's basketball book.

"You like the game?"

Jason shrugged his shoulders. "Basketball? Sort of. You need to be tall, though."

"Used to play a bit myself," said Sky. "How tall you are isn't as important as you think."

"'And zebras z-z-z-z-d!'" Earl interrupted, proudly snapping his book shut.

"Pretty good reading," said Sky. "What grade are you in, kid?"

Earl stared at Sky but didn't say anything.

"He's not allowed to talk to strangers," explained Jason.

"Good idea," Sky said.

"Tell him," Earl whispered in Jason's ear.

"It's all right, you can tell him yourself," said Jason.

"I'm in kinnergarden!" exclaimed Earl. "And I know my ABC's all the way to the end and halfway backward. Also two and two makes four and yellow and blue makes green. And Christopher Columbus surprised America. Jace told me."

"Not bad," said Sky. "You're way ahead of the game already. Like man, take our friend Puffy here," he said, picking up one of Earl's books. "It looks like he was so busy doing his bear number, he forgot to learn how to swim when he should have."

Sky turned to the end of the book, where Puffy Bear sat on top of a giant blue wave, holding up his umbrella triumphantly. "But look at him now! I guess it's never too late to learn something." Sky sighed, as if he didn't believe it himself.

"That's my favorite part!" said Earl. "Read it to me?"

Sky didn't say anything, but his neck got red. Jason wanted to ask him why he was just learning how to read, but he didn't know what words to use.

"I used to read to Earl all the time when I was just learning. It's good practice," Jason said, hoping Sky wasn't offended because he had figured out his problem. "And, anyway, Earl likes it when people read very slowly. He likes the story to last a long time."

"I do! A very long time, like one hundred minutes or something," agreed Earl.

"Maybe another time," Sky said.

When Sky, Jason, and Earl walked out of the library together, the dog on the stairs jumped up to lick Sky's face.

"I see that dog all the time," said Jason. "I didn't know he belonged to you until today."

Sky scratched the dog's head and behind his ears. "Old Lunch here thinks *I* belong to *him*. We found each other near the beach a few years ago."

"Lunch is a funny name for a dog," said Jason. He much preferred King himself.

"Well," said Sky, "when I first found him he was a wild little thing and would only come around at lunchtime."

"We only have a worm and a beetle and a birdie left," said Earl sadly. "Our pet snail got eaten."

Jason explained. "Our backyard belongs to the landlady's dog. She won't let us have a real pet of our own."

Sky nodded in an understanding way. "I know about landlords and landladies and their dogs and cats. But now old Lunch and I have the biggest backyard in the world," he said with a smile. "Front yard, too, don't we, boy?"

"Wow!" exclaimed Earl. "You must be very, very rich!"

"And getting richer every day," said Sky.

They were passing the basketball court. Sky picked up a stone. "Like I told you before, kid, height's not the most important thing. Practice is. And every time you face the hoop, just picture that ball in your mind, going right in. Picture first, then shoot!"

Sky stretched his tall frame toward the net and threw the stone straight in. "See ya, guys," he said, walking toward the bus stop.

"That man wasn't rich," Jason said when Sky was out of earshot.

"He said he was," said Earl.

"But his shirt had a tear in it," Jason pointed out.

"Maybe it's his favorite," said Earl, who had a Mickey Mouse T-shirt with holes in it that he liked to wear.

Suddenly Jason remembered what he had told Paul and Andrew. He was sorry he had called Sky a mean-looking varmint.

"Hey, next time I'll take your picture!" he called to Sky, but Lunch was barking and Sky didn't seem to hear him.

6

They started home, hurrying through the park and across the busy intersection at the light, stopping to buy a chocolate bearclaw and a cinnamon roll at the Donut Dunk. As usual, as soon as they passed the *Drink that Kids Love!* sign at the corner of Lemon Grove Avenue, Poopsie began barking.

Mrs. Raski opened her door a crack. "Shh!" she whispered. "Poopsie isn't himself and needs to rest quietly before dinner." She glanced disapprovingly at their doughnuts. "Plenty of additives in those!" she said, and shut the door.

Jason opened the Caputos' front door with his key and put the chain lock on when they got inside. Earl turned on the TV and the boys plopped down on the couch to watch "Captain Lightning's Interplanetary Adventures." During a commercial, Jason tried to call Mr. Hernandez once again, but his secretary, Judy, said he was in a meeting.

At six o'clock Mrs. Caputo rang her secret doorbell ring, two longs and one short. Jason buzzed her in to the building, and she came up the stairs. Jason opened the apartment door without taking the chain off.

"Password?" he asked.

"Spaghetti," she answered.

"You may enter," said Jason.

"How was school?" asked Mrs. Caputo.

"Okay," mumbled Jason, hoping she wouldn't ask any more questions.

"I want to hear all about it at dinner," said his mother on her way to the kitchen. "Now let's get to work."

Spaghetti suppers were Jason's favorite. The day before, the password had been hamburgers with mushrooms, Earl's favorite, for Mrs. Caputo was always fair. Spaghetti dinners took longer than hamburger dinners, but it was worth it when the sauce was finally ready. The Caputos had a routine. Earl opened the cans and set the table, Jason chopped the onions, and his mother did everything else.

Onions never made Jason cry. "Just like your dad," said Mrs. Caputo, tears sparkling in her eyes when she came near Jason's chopped onion pile. "Something you've inherited, I guess."

"And I 'herited red hair and freckles," Earl reminded her.

"That you did," said Mrs. Caputo.

Jason wished he had inherited something like that. People often stopped Earl to ask where he got his red hair, and Earl always said, "My dad, who died." Jason wished he had inherited something that didn't have to wait until you made spaghetti sauce for your mom to remark on it. Still, the idea thrilled Jason that a part of one person could be inside another, even if one of the persons was no longer around. He chopped an extra onion with a flourish because doing so made him feel good.

"Now, how was your first day at school?" asked his mom when they sat down to eat.

The fateful question, thought Jason. The big red D minus on his test paper fairly pulsed through the nylon of his knapsack. She would have to see it, he realized.

"Well," Jason answered, intently swirling a long strand of spaghetti around his fork, "my teacher's called Mean Lean McFeen. That should answer your question."

Mrs. Caputo put down her own fork. "No, frankly, it doesn't. It brings up more questions. What do you mean, 'mean'? Does she whip kids? Does she tie them up in closets if they make a mistake?"

"No," said Jason.

Earl giggled. "You're just being silly, Mommy," he said.

"Yes, I am," she said. "But when I was in school we sometimes called strict teachers 'mean'—

teachers who expected us to do our best and were stern when we didn't."

"Miss McFeen is like that," admitted Jason. He got up and brought his mother the test paper to be signed. May as well get it over with.

"And she's a very hard grader," he said.

His mother looked at the paper and sighed. "You were daydreaming again, I suppose," she said.

Jason nodded. Telling her about the letter to Mikey was, of course, out of the question.

"About the usual stuff? Spies and robbers and international rings?"

Jason shrugged. His mother looked at him for a few moments. Her eyes had blue eye-makeup shadows on top to match her blouse, but Jason knew that the pale gray shadows underneath meant that she was tired.

"I'm not sure what to do," she said softly.

That night Jason lay in his bunk bed, thinking. Below him, in the bottom bunk, Earl's snores gurgled softly. It had been a rotten day. A strict teacher, a D minus, a classmate who called him names. Three thousand miles away and three hours forward, Mikey was already snoring away, too. Jason looked out the window at the moon and the stars and felt small and alone.

Jason's mother came into the room. She bent down to check on Earl.

"That's the last D minus you'll ever see," Jason whispered.

"I hope so," said Mrs. Caputo.

Then Jason thought of something he had been meaning to ask for a while. "Mom, was Dad tall? I forget."

His mother leaned over the top bunk, smiling. "He was," she said. "But he started off short. Like you." Then she smoothed the blankets over Jason's shoulders and touched his cheek with her own. "Hey, Jace, daydreaming is wonderful. It's been the basis for some very fine actions. As long as you don't miss too much of the real world while you're doing it, honey." At the doorway she turned and said, "Sleep tight, okay?"

"Okay," said Jason. No more chasing figments of his imagination. This time he meant it.

Still, there *was* one story, one case worth looking into right away. Something real, something bothersome, something that would bring a small measure of comfort to his hardworking mom, not to mention Mr. Hernandez. Jason got out of bed, set his watch-alarm for 5:00 A.M., and added a few lines to Mikey's letter.

P.S. I am now investigating some neighborhood newspaper thieves.

I would really like to hear about what's happening with you. They call my teacher Mean Lean McFeen. Who did you get this year? Some kids in my new school are nicer than others.

P.P.S. My mom sends her best regards.

7

After a while it wasn't as much fun to see Mikey's familiar loopy handwriting on the outside of an envelope. Mikey peppered Jason with questions. "What's up? Broken any more news stories? How do you get to be a junior photojournalist, anyway? Is it something special in L.A.? Write back. ASAP. I promise to keep it confidential."

"How nice that you boys are maintaining your friendship by mail," remarked Mrs. Caputo. "But maybe you should start thinking about inviting some new friends over one Saturday or Sunday. They can even sleep over. We'll rent movies and have a barbecue."

"Mrs. Raski would complain about the noise if I did that," said Jason.

"I'm not so sure," said his mother. "I think she's getting used to having kids around."

Jason had to agree. Mrs. Raski still banged on her ceiling and came upstairs to complain when they blared the TV. She still peeked out the window when she heard Jason and Earl go by. But she had taken to baking chocolate-chip cookies for

Jason and Earl to eat every day after school. She used to make them for her own sons a long time ago, she had told Jason the first time she gave him and Earl the cookies.

"And with no additives like the sweets at the Donut Dunk," she had said.

It was strange to think of Mrs. Raski once living with a regular family instead of a crabby old dog.

"What if Poopsie attacked one of my friends?" Jason asked. "We could be sued."

"Oh, Jace," said his mother. "Poopsie wouldn't attack anybody."

"Oh, yeah?" said Jason, without going into any details.

Of course, the real reason for not inviting friends over was the bubble-gum bubble of a lie he had told about being an official junior photojournalist in training. What if his mother gave him away? His lie was getting hard to live with.

Jason knew he needed to solve the case of the missing newspapers in a hurry. Then at least *one* of his lies would no longer be a lie. He planned to take a picture of the newspaper thief, or thieves, if it turned out to be a criminal ring. He would show the photos to Mr. Hernandez. A stakeout would be organized on Lemon Grove Avenue, the thieves easily captured. He could even imagine the newspaper headline: Ring of Newspaper Thieves Disbanded! Story and photos by Jace Caputo.

"You were right, Al," Jason would say. "The camera never lies."

"Great story, Jace," Al would reply gratefully. "A wallapallooza."

For several days, Jason had been getting up at 5:00 A.M. to record the crime on film, but no thief or ring of thieves had slunk up their front walk. When Mrs. Caputo opened the door to retrieve the newspaper, it was right where it was supposed to be.

"I'm glad I phoned the newspaper to complain," she said. "I told you it was just an administrative error."

But one morning Jason sleepily turned off his watch-alarm by mistake and went back to sleep. The newspaper was missing at breakfast time!

"It's a thief, I'm sure of it," Jason informed his mother. "A clever one, at that."

The next day, in the early-morning darkness, Jason sat by his window. The *Drink that Kids Love!* sign blinked brightly high above the street corner, offering a clear view of Lemon Grove Avenue. Soon the newspaper delivery man drove up in his car. The man threw the paper out the car window

onto their front porch. Jason waited for something to happen, pen poised above his notebook, camera and flash at the ready. Several cars drove by. A man jogged around the corner and down the street, but didn't stop. At 7:00 A.M. he heard his mom open the door.

"Drat," she said, "missing again!"

Jason, still sitting by the window in his pajamas, was amazed! He hadn't seen a soul! How could that be? Ghosts? Chemical disintegration? No, he said to himself. It was simply that the thief was even more clever than he'd thought. This was a real mystery. At last. Mr. Hernandez would be very, very interested.

That day in class, Miss McFeen assigned a research paper on a scientific topic of local interest.

"You may use any visual aids you like. Pictures and maps and photographs, especially if you have access to a camera," Miss McFeen had said, pointedly looking at Jason, who was yawning sleepily.

After school Jason and Earl went to the library so that Jason could research his assignment. Paul and Andrew were there, too. Jason couldn't decide whether to do his report on earthquakes or the Pacific coast and had taken out books on both.

"Kids from other states always do reports on

earthquakes," said Andrew, pointing to the earthquake books Jason had checked out. "Kids who were born here are used to earthquakes. We get them all the time."

Jason decided then and there to do his report on the Pacific coast. In any case, it would be easier to photograph.

"*You've* done reports on earthquakes, and *you* were born here," said Paul to Andrew.

Andrew shrugged. "That was last year," he said.

"You're so lucky you know how to work a camera," Paul said to Jason. "It will probably help you get a better grade on your report."

Andrew frowned. "Hey, when do you train with this Mr. Hernandez, anyway?" he asked.

"Oh, whenever," said Jason vaguely.

Just then Sky entered the library. Jason guiltily pretended not to see him, but he noticed that Sky had shaved and gotten a haircut.

"There's that mysterious guy you're supposed to be investigating," said Andrew.

"Shh," said Jason, hoping Sky hadn't heard. "It's confidential."

Sky came over to their table. "I'm ready whenever you're ready to take my picture, kid. Got the old locks shorn, as you can see!"

Jason pulled his camera from his knapsack, and he and Sky went outside. Sky smiled broadly into the camera. "Mom will love this," he said.

"What do you know about him so far?" whispered Paul when they had returned and Sky had sat down at a table close by.

Jason reluctantly pulled his notebook from his pocket and found his notes on Sky. "Day after day, at four o'clock sharp," he whispered, "suspect meets with accomplice for thirty minutes. They work on code called the Big Twenty-six. Just beginning to crack it."

"Since when does someone you're confidentially investigating come over and ask to have his picture taken? Something fishy's going on here," said Andrew.

At four o'clock sharp, John Evans sat down beside Sky. "Ready to crack the code, Sky?" he asked, pulling some books and papers from his briefcase.

"Wow," said Paul.

When Mr. Evans left, Earl went over to Sky and pulled at his blue shirt. "Mister, it's another time," he said. He put a big pile of books on the table.

"Another time?" asked Sky.

"Uh-huh. You said you'd read to me another

time. Jace is working on his report."

Miss Whitestreet was replacing books on a shelf nearby. Without turning around, she said, "You can do it, Sky."

Sky's neck got red, but he said, "Well, I guess it'll be good practice like your big brother told me." Earl sat down beside Sky and opened a book. "Okay, kid, let's shoot a few baskets," said Sky. And, haltingly, he began to read.

Jason pretended not to listen, but he couldn't help hearing. Sky figured out words the way Jason remembered doing a long time ago, even as far back as first grade. Letters were sounded out one by one, then mumbled together quickly to see what happened, then again, in joyful surprise, to make a real word.

At first Sky read quietly, until Earl told him he couldn't hear. After a while he read a little louder, and Jason noticed that his neck wasn't as red. "I'm doing better than I thought I would," said Sky in a surprised voice when he had finished the story. He closed the book and slapped its front cover with his large hand. "Great story!"

"Again," said Earl.

Jason motioned Andrew and Paul to follow him to the other side of the room. "Earl's working undercover," he said quietly.

Andrew looked very suspicious. He began muttering under his breath and counting on his fingers. "X. Twenty-four. Y. Twenty-five. Z. Twenty-six. Hey! Now I get it! Code Big Twenty-six is nothing but the alphabet! What's the big deal? All that guy's doing is learning how to read!"

"Well, who said learning to read isn't a big deal?" said Jason defiantly.

"You're no junior photojournalist. I've never even heard of that!" Andrew exclaimed.

"Oh, yes I am!"

"Bet you're not really working on any old case!"

"Bet I am!"

"I bet Mr. Hernandez doesn't even know you!"

"Bet he does!"

"Bet he doesn't!"

"Bet he does!"

"Would you really bet on it?"

"Sure!"

"I'll bet my basketball against your camera that Mr. Hernandez doesn't know you from a hole in the wall!"

Jason paused. He hadn't expected that.

"See?" gloated Andrew. "You're afraid to bet!"

There was nothing to worry about, thought Jason. Mr. Hernandez had taken his picture just that summer! And not only that, Jason's were some of the phone calls Mr. Hernandez had to return but just hadn't gotten around to yet because of his very busy schedule. If they went straight to the offices of the *West L.A. Public Weekly* right then and there, Jason could save Mr. Hernandez a phone call. He had been meaning to drop in, anyway. And now Jason would be able to give him a personal report about the mysterious disappearance of his own publication. Mr. Hernandez would really appreciate that!

"It's a deal," said Jason.

Andrew looked surprised. "You mean you'd really give me your camera?"

"I would," said Jason. "But I know I won't have to. Mr. Hernandez knows me."

"Prove it!" said Andrew.

8

Jason took Mr. Hernandez's card from his pocket. He quietly asked Miss Whitestreet to look up the address on a Los Angeles street map.

"That's three blocks west toward the ocean and two blocks east on Cilantro Avenue," she said.

Jason, Andrew, Paul, and Earl walked the five blocks to the newspaper office, a low-slung brick building with glass doors that said *The West L.A. Public Weekly* on the front.

Jason pushed open the heavy doors, his heart pounding.

Inside, the air conditioning was crisp and cool. Computers clicked, teletype machines clattered, phones rang. Men and women at their desks, some with pencils behind their ears, busily concentrated on the news of the day, typing, talking on the telephone, drinking coffee. It was a place of action. It was just as Jason had imagined it!

"I'm Jason Caputo, junior photojournalist," he announced to the pretty young woman at the front desk. "I'd like to speak to Mr. Al Hernandez, please. Here to discuss a case."

"Why, it's Jace the Ace! At last! I'm Judy," she said, laughing. "Have a seat. I'll tell Al you're here."

"Wow," said Paul.

The boys sat down on a long bench. Jason listened with relief and anticipation as Judy spoke into the intercom.

"A Mr. Caputo to see you, Al," she said.

A voice murmured back at her through the machine.

"Al's in a very important meeting," Judy said. "He may be awhile."

"We'll wait," said Jason, looking smugly at Andrew, who seemed to be holding his basketball more tightly.

They waited and waited. Judy offered them cold cups of water, peppermint candies, and souvenir W.L.A.P.W. pencils. Andrew took a newspaper from a stack of papers, and the three older boys took turns acting out their favorite characters from the comics page, trying to make the others guess who they were. Jason looked at his watch. He had been enjoying himself so much he hadn't realized that thirty whole minutes had gone by.

"I have to go," said Paul.

Jason asked Judy if she could please buzz Mr. Hernandez again. She did, and suddenly an angry

voice crackled back loudly over the intercom.

"Is that the kid who calls me on the phone all the time?"

Judy frowned and spoke low into the intercom.

"Hey, Judy, I don't care how cute they are! You know how I am when I've got a deadline to make!"

Judy looked up at Jason and shrugged her shoulders. "I'm really sorry, Jason," she said.

"I knew it!" said Andrew, as the boys left. "He doesn't know you from a hole in the wall!"

Jason's eyes filled up with tears. "Gee, I'm not an *official* photojournalist, but I really did think he'd remember me," he said.

The boys were quiet on the walk back, except for Earl. Jason knew Earl had been too busy reading with Sky when the bet was made and didn't really understand the awful thing that had just happened. Earl skipped along, singing songs from school, calling out every now and then, whenever he thought he saw Captain Lightning.

When they reached the library Andrew said, "I guess you can keep your camera a little longer. At least until you finish your roll of film."

"Thanks," said Jason, turning quickly toward home, hoping Andrew and Paul couldn't see the tears in his eyes.

"That man in the machine didn't have very nice

manners, did he, Jace?" commented Earl, taking Jason's hand and running to keep up.

Jason didn't answer. Tears were running down his cheeks. How could he ever have imagined that Mr. Hernandez was his friend? That he was his partner on assignment? Actually, that's all he had been doing. Imagining. Making up stuff. Worse, lying about it. And now he had lost his camera. Jason let go of Earl's hand and began to walk even faster.

"Hey, wait up!" cried Earl.

But didn't Mr. Hernandez remember that day in the summer? thought Jason. "Jason," he had said. "A go-getter like yourself needs a go-getter name. Jace the Ace. What do you think?"

"Are you crying?" asked Earl, running beside him.

"No," Jason said.

"You are!" said Earl. "I see tears."

"I'm chopping onions," said Jason, slowing down.

Earl put his arm around Jason. "Don't cry, Jace," he said.

"I can't help it," said Jason, wiping his eyes with the palm of his hand.

"I know how you feel," said Earl. "I know how you feel when you can't help it."

It was later than usual. The *Drink that Kids Love!* sign was already blinking in the dusk. But something else was different, too. Poopsie wasn't barking the way he usually did when they turned the corner down Lemon Grove Avenue.

Mrs. Raski opened her door as the boys climbed the front steps. "You're late, boys. I was worried about you," she said.

"We had a long day," said Jason.

"So did I," said Mrs. Raski. Then Jason noticed that Mrs. Raski looked as if she'd been crying, too.

"Poopsie died early this morning," she said sadly. "It was his heart."

Then Mrs. Raski went inside and came out again with a big box. "Please give these to your mom," she said, her voice quavering. "I was cleaning out poor Poopsie's dog house, and I found them piled up inside. Tell her I'm very sorry. They're outdated, but maybe she can find a use for them."

The box was filled with old newspapers. Stolen copies of the *West L.A. Public Weekly.*

"He must have dragged them into the backyard every now and then when he went out to do his early morning business," said Mrs. Raski, lovingly stroking a yellowed newspaper. "Poor old dear. He just wasn't himself toward the end. He is gone,

but the backyard will be his forever."
Poopsie had struck again.

Dear Mikey,
    I am working on my report, so I won't be able to write to you for a long, long time.
Jason

9

That Sunday Jason, Earl, Mrs. Caputo, and Mrs. Raski went to the beach. Jason planned to go on a hike along the shore to research his report on the Pacific coast.

"Perfect weather," said Mrs. Caputo. She spread a big striped towel on the sand and sat down on it. "Not too hot and not too cool."

Mrs. Raski, blinking back tears, sat down on the towel beside her. "Yes, this is lovely," she said. "But I can't help thinking about poor Poopsie, cooped up in a grave. Oh, how I miss him!"

Mrs. Caputo patted her arm. "Now, now, Bertha. Being with friends on a beautiful day like this will help fill the void," she said. "You've been spending much too much time indoors mourning Poopsie."

Outdoors, too, thought Jason. He was glad he was going for a hike on the beach because Mrs. Raski talked about Poopsie all the time. But he did feel sorry for her. He knew how it felt to miss someone terribly, especially someone who had died.

Jason sadly put his camera around his neck, making sure the lens cover was on securely for protection from sandy breezes. He still took excellent care of the camera, even though today was to be the very last day he would ever use it. As soon as he finished this roll of film for his report on the Pacific coast, the camera would belong to Andrew. He had lied about being an official junior photojournalist, and he had been found out. In the end he would be a boy of his word.

Jason vowed then and there that his last pictures would be his best pictures ever! His head was full of all the things he had been reading about in his library book, *Seashore Life of the Great Pacific Coast.*

"Can I come with you, Jace?" asked Earl, picking up his pail and shovel. "Please? I'm a very good hiker."

"No, you're not," said Jason. "You always poop out."

"But that was before I was in kinnergarden," said Earl.

"You haven't been in kindergarten very long. You couldn't have changed *that* much."

"Yes, I have!" protested Earl. "I'm a better runner, and I can read a little bit!"

Jason sighed. He could probably use an extra pair of eyes. "Oh, okay, come on," he said. "I guess you can help me." Jason flipped through the pages of his library book. "This is what we have to look for. Golden sand dunes. Mud-rock caverns. Sea gulls and flatworms and octopi and crabs. Tide pools. Maybe a gray whale or dolphin far out to sea."

"Okay," said Earl cheerfully. "I can put some animals in my pail."

"Oh, no," said Jason. "We're not going to disturb nature's beauty. All I'm going to do is take pictures."

"All right," said Earl.

Mrs. Caputo smeared sunblock on Earl and told Jason to put some on, too. Jason filled his canteen with water for the hike, and packed it in his knapsack with his library book, his little notebook and pencil, and some sandwiches and tangerines. Then they waved good-bye and started on their way.

"Keep a good eye on Earl," called Mrs. Caputo. "And don't go farther than the pier!"

They trudged along the shore. Jason looked around. It certainly wasn't like the Great Pacific Coast of his library book. Yelling bathers, not dolphins, jumped the waves. There were sea gulls, but they were running in and out of the crowds, looking annoyed.

"This isn't what I had in mind," Jason muttered. He snapped a picture of a sea gull dragging a half-eaten sandwich along the paper-strewn sand. "I thought there would be better things to photograph!"

They walked on. A small crowd had gathered farther down the shore. Jason and Earl stopped to see what the commotion was about. Two men in bathing suits, the muscles in their arms rippling, their faces red and sweaty, were standing on their heads.

"They've been standing on their heads for five hours, since the sun rose," said a man to Jason and Earl. "Both trying to get into the *Guinness Book of World Records.*"

A girl fed each man some canned juice through long straws and wiped their brows with a handkerchief. One of the men began to sway back and forth, his strong legs straight up in the air looking like a tall tree about to fall down. The crowd *ooh*ed and *aah*ed, seeming to sway with him until he caught his balance again.

"Close call," said the man, smiling an upside-down smile at everybody.

Jason was just about to snap their picture when he thought better of it. "Wasted shot. Let's go, Earl," he said.

"Oh, darn," said Earl, trudging behind him in the sand. "I wanted to see them break a world record! And that would have made a good picture, Jace."

"I need pictures for my Pacific coast report, not the circus," said Jason.

"Oh," said Earl.

They walked on. Jason counted two Frisbee games, one volleyball game, and three sand castles. The people were too numerous to count. There wasn't an octopus or a mud-rock cavern or a gray whale in sight!

He sat down on the sand, pulling out his notebook and pencil and their lunch from his knapsack. Earl sat down beside him.

Jason scribbled down what they had seen so far. It wasn't much, he thought. He felt hot, tired, and very sorry for himself as he contemplated a D minus, or worse, on his report. He ran through all his other miseries in his mind. There were quite a few. Losing his camera, of course. Mr. Hernandez's forgetting him. Missing his good buddy and not being able to write to him, what with all the lies he had told. And no dog to help him feel better. No dog in his near future, either, as long as their backyard was a memorial for Poopsie!

Jason watched a girl step into a sand hole and cover herself with sand.

"You should take a picture of *that*!" exclaimed Earl. "She's buried all the way up to her neck!"

"Not scientific enough," said Jason.

They finished their sandwiches and their tangerines and threw the trash into a garbage pail.

"See ya," sang the girl in the sand.

"I bet you're going to break a world record!" said Earl admiringly.

"Broke it yesterday," said the girl.

Ahead of them loomed the pier. The waves crashed white and frothy against the thick, treelike poles supporting it. The shoreline path underneath the pier was dark and spooky. They had come to the end of their Pacific coast hike.

"Phooey!" said Jason. "Now we have to turn around, and all I got was a picture of a sea gull eating a sandwich!"

Earl squinted out to sea. "I think I see a whale, Jace," he said.

Jason looked, too, but didn't see anything.

"You're imagining things," he said.

Music filtered down from the pier above. "Playland." Earl read slowly from the big sign overhead. "Look! A playland, Jace! Let's go see!"

They climbed the stairs. There, at the top, was an arcade. The music was coming from a lovely carousel whose brightly painted horses danced around and around. People were laughing and eating and trying to win prizes. Jason didn't have enough money for rides or games, but he was able to buy two cinnamon rolls to share with Earl.

"Look, Jace! Take a picture of that boy winning a giant panda!" cried Earl, his mouth full of food.

That made Jason remember his report again. "Oh, darn!" he said. "I don't have any good pictures at all, and we have to start back now."

"Look, Jace! Over there! Take a picture!"

"Don't be a weirdo, Earl!" said Jason in an exasperated voice. "Miss McFeen doesn't want to see pictures of a boy winning a prize or a girl buried in the sand or two men standing on their heads. She wants to see pictures of the Pacific coast," said Jason.

"Look, Jace!" cried Earl again.

Jason was staring up at the clouds. He thought they looked like white whales and dolphins frolicking in a blue sea.

"This will have to do," he said, sighing. He snapped pictures of the sky with its oddly shaped clouds, and the crowded beach teeming with bathers. "Let's go now, Earl," he said.

But when Jason turned around, Earl was nowhere to be seen.

10

"Earl, come on!" Jason shouted angrily.

He looked to the left and to the right. He saw the jostling crowds strolling up and down the pier, all strangers, none of them Earl.

"Earl, where are you?" Jason shouted. "We have to go!"

But Earl had disappeared. Jason's heart started pounding. He began to retrace his steps.

"Did you see a short kid around kindergarten age with red hair and freckles?" he asked a fat man at the doughnut stand. "He ordered a cinnamon roll a little while ago. Maybe he ordered another one?"

But the fat man shook his head. "Can't say that I did," he said. "Anyway, you kids all look the same to me. Sorry!"

Jason ran to the stand where he and Earl had seen people knocking down bottles to win a prize. A small group was watching a girl try to win. Jason looked at everyone, hoping to see Earl cheering good-naturedly. But his brother wasn't there.

In the distance, Jason heard the carousel's song.

"That's where he is!" he said aloud, racing down the pier. Jason scrutinized all the riders on the carousel. Around and around and around they went. A boy with a cowboy hat, a man, a woman, a girl with a doll. The boy with the cowboy hat again. None of them a boy with red hair and freckles. None of them Earl. Jason watched until he felt dizzy. Finally, he turned and continued running.

"Earl! Where are you?" he cried.

A man was fishing over the side of the pier. Fish were swimming in a big pail by his chair. Earl loved fish! Maybe he'd stopped to have a look.

"Have you seen a boy with red hair?" Jason asked. "He had a pail, too. And a shovel, for scooping up sand."

But the man shrugged his shoulders and said something in Spanish.

With his hand Jason tried to show the man how short Earl was, coming up to Jason's chest. The man shook his head. Either he still didn't understand or he hadn't seen him—Jason couldn't figure out which.

From the pier Jason saw the waves below sweeping along the shore. A terrible, terrible thought occurred to him. Earl was just learning how to swim! Had he been swept out to sea?

But there! There he was, walking slowly by the

shore! Jason ran down the wooden stairs as fast as he could.

"Earl! Earl!" he cried. "Wait up! Where're you going?"

The boy turned around. It wasn't Earl.

"Did you see a boy about your size walk by?" Jason asked him.

"I'm five," said the boy proudly.

"Yes, but did you see my brother? He has red hair," said Jason.

"I didn't see *your* brother," said the little boy. "I saw *my* brother, but he doesn't have red hair. My teacher has red hair!"

Jason felt like crying. "Thanks," he said, running past him. "Earl, where are you?" he cried as he ran.

At the edge of the sand was a steep cliff, with stone stairs going up to a bridge that crossed the busy freeway. The bridge led to a grassy area where many people strolled and walked their dogs on leashes. Jason trudged up the stairs and over the bridge. He swerved in and out among bike riders and joggers and all the Sunday strollers, hoping against hope to see a five-year-old red-haired boy patting a dog. But Earl was nowhere to be seen.

Tears streamed down his cheeks. Jason could

hardly see in front of him, and his breath came in short gasps. Suddenly he heard a dog barking excitedly.

"Whoa there, my friend! Where's the fire?"

To Jason's surprise, the voice was familiar. And so was the bark. There, before him, were Sky and his dog, Lunch.

"Sky!" Jason cried. "I've lost my brother, Earl! I've looked everywhere for him. Have you seen him?"

Sky frowned. "I haven't seen him," he said. "Where did you see him last?"

"On the pier down on the beach! I turned around and he was gone!"

"Let's go back down and ask a lifeguard to help us," said Sky gently.

Sky and Jason went over the bridge and down to the beach again, with Lunch leading the way. In the distance, Jason could see the shiny colors of the arcade. He heard the cheerful music of the carousel. But under the pier it was dark and spooky, and the waves splashed high against the supporting poles. Jason shivered, thinking the very worst. Kidnapped! Swept out to sea! Possible things that could happen, not just imaginings! He took Sky's hand.

"Earl! Earl!" Jason shouted, the sound of his

voice mingling with Lunch's barks.

And then, as they approached the pier, he heard someone calling. Jason ran closer to the pier and looked up.

There was Earl, looking down. Earl, his face tear-stained and dirty, his red hair glinting in the sunlight, waving and calling Jason's name. Earl, his absolute best buddy on either the Atlantic coast or the Pacific coast. In the whole wide world, in fact. Good old Earl!

Jason ran up the wooden stairs and hugged his brother. He couldn't remember ever being happier to see anyone in his entire life.

"Oh, Jace! Oh, Sky! Lunch! Thank you for finding me!" Earl began to sob.

Sky grinned and looked relieved. Lunch licked Earl's face.

"I was chasing after Captain Lightning!" cried Earl. "I wanted to get his autograph as a surprise for you, Jace, and then maybe you could also take his picture! I ran and ran and he went into a restaurant called Eats and I followed him and he sat down to eat his lunch and when I looked up close it wasn't even him! And so then I came out of the restaurant and I was lost and so were you!"

Jason felt his knees shaking. "That was very nice of you," he said. "I know you were trying to make me feel better."

"I was!" said Earl, still sobbing. "I wanted you to get a picture of something good so you could give it to mean Miss McFeen!"

"Oh, Earl," said Jason. "Sometimes a person's mind plays dirty tricks on him. Sometimes a person wants something so much he thinks he can see it."

Earl nodded his head vigorously, his sobs subsiding.

Jason felt so ashamed. His brother had been lost and it had really been his fault. Something terrible could have happened!

"The very same thing happened to me when I ran after Captain Lightning that time in the park," said Jason. "Remember? But *I* did something worse than just imagine. I said I'd really seen something when I knew for sure I really hadn't."

"Why did you do that?" asked Earl.

Jason thought for a moment. "I guess I wanted to feel big," he said.

"But you *are* big!" said Earl. "You're a fifth grader!"

"You're such a weirdo," said Jason, putting his arm around his brother.

"Well, now," said Sky softly. "Someone's probably looking for *both* of you by now. Probably worried that you guys went off with Puffy Bear and the big wave!"

Earl giggled and took Sky's hand. They all walked off the pier and across the sand, with Lunch leading the way.

"Old Lunch and I have to go back now," said Sky, when they neared the stairs to the bridge beyond the beach. He whistled a tune and Lunch ran to his side. "Dogs aren't allowed on the sand, you know."

"Thanks for helping me find Earl," said Jason.

"You bet," said Sky. Then he smiled a big, wide smile, so wide it made the scar-arrow above his eye disappear into his eyebrow. "Come by the library next Sunday," he said. "One week from today at twelve noon. Sharp. I have a surprise for both of you."

"But the library is closed on Sunday!" said Jason.

"Next Sunday is special," said Sky. "You'll see!"

Then Sky and Lunch climbed the stairs up the cliffs overlooking the ocean, to the other side. "Lunch has the biggest backyard in the world. Front yard, too," Sky had said. And now Jason understood what that meant.

Jason and Earl quietly walked back along the shore. Jason took a picture of a man jogging on the wet sand with a big, green parrot perched on his shoulder. He snapped another of a girl doing somersaults on a blanket.

Suddenly something strange began to happen. The ground beneath their feet began to shake gently.

"What is it?" asked Earl in a quivering voice.

"Earthquake," said Jason, taking his hand.

So this is what it's like! he thought. Just as he'd read in the library books. But there were no tidal waves as far as he could see, and nothing was tumbling down. There was just the shaking, like a big subway train rumbling by.

"I'm scared, Jace," said Earl.

"Don't be afraid," Jason said. "The earth is just shifting its crust a little bit."

Soon the shaking stopped. Some people seemed unaware that the ground had moved, and soon everybody continued swimming and eating and jogging and sunning, as if nothing unusual had happened.

"I'll bet it wasn't even a four point zero on the Richter scale," said the man with the parrot on his shoulder. The bird itself looked unperturbed.

"I can read you some books about earthquakes," said Jason. "Then we can make an earthquake preparation box and help Mom and Mrs. Raski make our house earthquake-proof."

"Good," said Earl. "I'm not so scared anymore."

Jason took a picture of Earl standing bravely on the shore. "For my report," he said.

Then he snapped a picture of the two men who were still standing on their heads and one of some sea gulls flying by.

What a hike! Earl getting lost and meeting Sky and Lunch and feeling an earthquake! Jason felt as if he had crossed the universe and returned.

11

"Very nice pictures," said Mrs. Caputo the following Sunday.

She held up the photograph of Sonia and Mary Anne, the Serenading Sitter Sisters. "Such lovely girls!" she exclaimed. "But why do they wear their hair poking out from the side of the head like that?"

"Show business," said Jason, examining the developed pictures, fresh from the photo-processing store. The camera never lies, he thought ruefully. There were the scenes of crimes that never were, the beach as it really was, Earl, Sky, Officer Jordan and Officer Brown, simply being themselves.

"Your father," said his mother dreamily, "your father took the most wonderful pictures of people! I'm going to dig them up for you to see. They're packed away in boxes. Some of them were so true and real he showed them only to me. Fat Aunt Lucy bending over the stove, Mr. Botticelli yacking away, everybody around him looking bored. Pictures of me . . ."

Mrs. Caputo stared out Jason's bedroom win-

dow as if she were seeing something far away but familiar. "I'll show you *some* of them," she said, blushing. "And the imaginative ones he did for fun!" she continued, laughing. "Close-ups of pickles, melons wearing spectacles, clouds that looked like other things."

She looked at Jason's pictures again. "I think you've inherited his imagination and talent," she said.

"Really?" exclaimed Jason delightedly.

"Really," said his mother, giving him a hug. "You just have to learn to dream at the right time and place, that's all."

Jason felt much better, even though he didn't have the nerve to tell his mother that he was about to lose his camera because of a bet. He had arranged to meet Andrew at the library that day. At least he would still have his dad's photography genes.

Earl came into the bedroom carrying some new goldfish in a bowl. "I'm taking my fish for a walk," he announced.

"Oh, honey!" said Mrs. Caputo. "You can't do that!"

"Yes, I can!" said Earl. "It's too boring for them, swimming around and around!"

"Hey, Earl," said Jason, selecting two photographs from his pile, one of Sky standing with Lunch and one of the Serenading Sitter Sisters. "We need to go to the library now. We can take your fish for a walk another time." He slipped his camera strap over his shoulder.

"Okay," said Earl.

Mrs. Raski opened her door as the boys went by. The smell of stew from her kitchen mingled with the scent of chocolate.

"Cookies will be ready soon!" she announced cheerfully.

Andrew was sitting on the library steps. Lunch was lying beside him.

"I see you brought it," he said, eyeing the camera.

"I told you I would. Here," said Jason sadly.

Andrew took the camera. "Nice," he said. He slowly put the strap over his shoulder and patted the case. Then he gave a big sigh. "I don't even know how to use a camera like this. My father doesn't really let me use his all the time. He never even lets me touch it."

"Really?" Jason hesitated, but then he said, "I know some good books you could check out of the library." He wanted Andrew to take good care of the camera.

Even though it was Sunday, a smiling Miss Whitestreet ushered Jason, Earl, and Andrew into the library. Just as Sky had promised, something unusual was happening inside. In a corner of the large room, a small audience was seated in front of a podium. And there on the sidelines was Mr. Hernandez with his camera. To Jason's surprise, Mr. Hernandez winked at him! Jason wondered what was going on.

"This is a very, very special occasion," said Miss Whitestreet, stepping behind the podium. She smiled broadly as Mr. Hernandez snapped a picture of her. "We are here to award California Literacy Certificates to the adult learners in our community, as well as Service Awards to the tutors who have helped them. What a wonderful job they have done!"

The audience clapped. Then Miss Whitestreet called up the adult learners and their tutors. Jason recognized several of them: the Rich Heiress, crying softly as she accepted her certificate and gave a little speech of thanks; the Counterintelligence Spy, who planted a big kiss on Miss Whitestreet's cheek; and Sky and Mr. Evans. Sky was all dressed up in a red shirt with green palm trees and yellow bananas on it. He stepped forward to give a speech.

"Thank you." Looking out at the audience proudly, Sky waited until the clapping had subsided. "When I was a young kid we moved around a lot," he said. "I found reading very hard, but I was ashamed to ask for help. I pretended I knew how to read. When I got older, I still pretended. I carried a newspaper around with me everywhere I went so that people would think I knew how to read it. Now I don't have to pretend anymore."

The audience clapped vigorously.

"Mr. Evans helped me. So did Miss Whitestreet. They had faith that I could do it." Sky peered out into the audience. "And there were two other great guys, library members, who helped me, too. I see that they're here today. Come up here, Jason and Earl!"

Everybody turned around to look. Jason hesitated, but Earl took his hand. "We're coming!" said Earl, pulling Jason forward.

"These guys made me practice," Sky continued, putting his arms around the boys' shoulders. "Jason helped me write a letter. I learned to read and write, but I also learned that I'm tired of being a ramblin' man. I don't have to pretend and be ashamed anymore. I miss my family and my friends. Mom sent me a ticket, in care of the library, and I'm going home to Wisconsin on the next plane, folks!"

The audience cheered as Sky waved his ticket in the air, smiling broadly.

"Well, what do you know?" exclaimed Mr. Hernandez. He snapped pictures of Sky shaking hands with Jason, Earl, Mr. Evans, and Miss Whitestreet. "This will make a wallapallooza of a human-interest story!"

Then Sky took a deep breath and leaned toward the audience again. "One more thing, folks. I have this dog, see. He likes to be near the ocean and smell the salty breezes, but where I'm going, there is no ocean. Anybody here know someone who can give him a good home and also take him for a walk near the beach every now and then?"

Jason looked at Earl. Earl looked at Jason. "We do!" they shouted.

12 _____

Sky, Jason, Earl, and Andrew walked out of the library together. There was Lunch, waiting for them. Jason could hardly believe it! Their very own dog!

"I have to go now, guys," said Sky. "I've got a plane to catch, and it'll take me a long time to get to the airport by bus."

Then Jason remembered the photograph he had brought for Sky. "This is for you," he said, handing it to him.

Sky stared at the photograph for several seconds. "It's a great picture," he said.

Jason noticed that Sky had tears in his eyes. Sky knelt down and enveloped Lunch in his arms. It looked as if he was whispering something in the dog's ear.

"All set," Sky said, standing up. "Remember now, whistle a bit of "The Star-Spangled Banner" or "Jingle Bells" during the day, "Taps" at night, okay?"

Jason tooted a few notes, but Earl blew vainly.

"I can't do it," Earl said unhappily.

"I'll give you some lessons," said Jason. "It'll be much easier when your teeth grow in."

"Even when your teeth grow in, guys, it's still a good idea to practice," said Sky, winking at Jason, "whether it's whistling, or reading a book, or just throwing the old basketball through the hoop."

Then Sky saw his bus and raced to catch it, waving good-bye as he ran.

"Good-bye! Don't forget to write!" Jason cried.

"Good-bye! Good-bye!" shouted Earl. "Thanks for our doggie!"

Jason and Earl and Andrew waved until the bus was out of sight.

Lunch got up and looked west after Sky. Jason whistled "The Star-Spangled Banner," and Lunch followed Jason instead. It was absolutely amazing.

Mr. Hernandez was getting into his van as the boys and Lunch walked by. "Hey, Jason," he said. "Sorry I was nasty the other day, but I'm an ogre when I've got a deadline to meet! Judy really chewed me out on that one. I worked with you this summer, right?"

"Right," said Jason.

"Okay, you win," said Andrew, giving the camera back.

"Well," said Jason, "I really wasn't an *official* junior photojournalist."

"I know," said Andrew. "But take it, anyway. I'd get in trouble because my parents would never in a million years believe that I won it in a bet!"

"Okay," said Jason happily. "Hey, what if I teach you about photography and you teach me how to dribble?"

"Deal," said Andrew, turning toward home.

Jason and Earl passed by the basketball court. Jason picked up a stone from the ground and imagined that the stone was a ball. He could see the ball sailing up, up toward the net, down, and in. He could even hear the roaring of the crowds, even though it was really only Earl cheering him on.

"Yay!" yelled Earl when the stone plopped into the net.

Jason felt ten feet tall. At least.

13

Lunch followed them all the way—toward Lemon Grove Avenue, under the *Drink that Kids Love!* sign, and around the block, where they found the Serenading Sitter Sisters crooning on the corner.

"Doo-dah, doo-dah," they sang, waving to Jason and Earl.

"Here's your picture," said Jason. "See? I was telling the truth about the film in my camera."

Sonia and Mary Anne looked it over. "I love our hair!" said Mary Anne.

"Thanks, Jace," said Sonia. "We could make copies of this for publicity and pin them up all around town. You're a good friend."

Jason whistled happily as he walked down the street with Lunch beside him. Earl blew, too, wetting his lips.

"I think I just heard something," Earl said delightedly. "A teeny, tiny peep."

Mrs. Raski was sitting on the front porch.

"Do you think she'll let us keep him?" Earl asked in a small voice.

"Leave it to me," said Jason, even though he was worried, too. But by the time they got close enough so he could hear the lonely squeak of her rocking chair, he knew it would be okay.

"This dog doesn't have a home, Mrs. Raski," Jason said as they turned up the walk.

Mrs. Raski stopped rocking. "Well," she said, looking Lunch over. Lunch wagged his tail. "Well," she said again. "Do you think he likes stew?"

"Probably," said Jason.

Mrs. Caputo came bounding down the stairs. Lunch barked, and Jason introduced them. Lunch licked her hand. Jason's mom sat down on the front stairs, put her chin in her hand, and sighed.

"Oh, Jace," she said. She had a stern and worried look that Jason had seen before, when he had brought home a note from his teacher or torn his good pants.

"Mrs. Raski said it was all right to keep him, Mom. Really," he said.

Mrs. Raski nodded. Earl took Jason's hand. They all waited.

"We'll discuss it," Mrs. Caputo said at last. "But that's not the problem. Jason, I just got a long-distance call from Mikey's mother. Who on *earth* is Uncle Seymour?"

Dear Mikey,

It was good to talk to you on the phone the other day.

I hope you will still be my friend even though you now know the truth. Mr. Hernandez, the photojournalist at the *West L.A. Public Weekly,* says the camera never lies. I guess the pen shouldn't, either.

Please write again. Maybe you can even come visit someday. We can go to Disneyland. You will meet my new buddies and our new dog, Lunch.

Enclosed is a clipping from the newspaper. Yes, I'm in the news again! As you can see from the picture, I'm a little bigger and Earl has more missing teeth. That tall guy standing with us is our friend Sky. You can read the interesting details about him in this newspaper article.

Things are pretty good around here. Hope they are for you, too! I got a B plus on my report, "Earthquakes Along the Pacific Coast." My teacher, Miss McFeen, a very hard grader, said it was both imaginative and realistic. She's not as mean as I thought she was.

Hey, would you believe me if I told you that Sky's full name is Skyler "Skyhook"

Madison, onetime top basketball player for the Milwaukee Bucks?

I guess you won't, and I don't blame you.

I remain,
Your old buddy,
Jace the Ace